Aladdin
and the
Wonderful
Lamp

by ANNE TERRY WHITE

illustrated by VERA BOCK

LEGACY

~9483

BOOKS

RANDOM HOUSE · NEW YORK

J
398
w

12-15-59

Manufactured in the United States of America

The Long-Lost Uncle

In a city of China there lived a poor tailor who had an only son, called Aladdin. Now this boy was from his babyhood a scamp and a good-for-nothing.

When Aladdin was ten years old, his father took him into his shop. But the lad would not learn tailoring. No, he would not sit in the shop for a single day. As soon as his father turned his back, Aladdin would run off and go to the gardens with the other scamps, his low companions. Scolding and punishment did no good. And presently, because of grief over his boy, the tailor sickened and died.

Seeing that her son was good for nothing at all, the widow sold the shop. She fell to spinning cotton yarn. And by this work she fed herself and her son. But Aladdin only grew more idle every day. He would stay home only at meal times. And so it went on, for both the mother and the boy, till Aladdin had reached his fifteenth year.

One day as he was playing with the gutter boys, behold! a stranger came up and stood looking hard at Aladdin. Now this stranger was a Moorman from Inner Morocco. And he was a powerful Magician.

"Verily," the Magician said to himself after looking at Aladdin, "this is the lad I need. This is he whom I have left my native land to find."

So presently he led one of the children apart and asked him about the boy. "What is his name? Whose son is he?" And when he had found out, he walked up to Aladdin and took him aside.

"O my son," the Magician said, "perchance you are the son of Such-an-one the tailor?"

"Yes, O my lord," the lad answered, "but 'tis long since he died."

At this the Moorman threw himself upon Aladdin and began kissing him and weeping. "I am your father's brother," he said. "I have come home after long exile in the hope of looking upon him once more. And now you tell me he is dead. O my son, I have only you to grieve with me now."

So saying, the Magician with many tears put his hand to his purse and took out ten gold pieces. And he gave them to the lad. "O my son," he said, "where is your house? And where lives your mother, my brother's widow?"

Aladdin showed him the way to their home. Then the Wizard said: "O my son, give these moneys to your mother,

2

The stranger looked hard at Aladdin

and let her know that your uncle, your father's brother, has come from exile. On the morrow I will visit her and eat the evening meal with you."

Aladdin kissed the stranger's hand and ran home as fast as he could.

"O my son," the widow said when she heard the tale, "you mock me. Well I know you had an uncle, but he is now dead. Nor am I aware that you had another one."

All the same, she arose at once, and going to the market street, bought all she required. Then she borrowed from the neighbors whatever was needed of pans and platters and so forth.

The next day when the evening meal was cooked and suppertime came, she said to Aladdin: "O my child, the meat is ready. Go forth and meet your uncle on the road."

"To hear is to obey," he replied.

But they had not ended talking when a knock was heard at the door. Aladdin went out and opened. And behold! the Magician came in together with a servant carrying wine and fruits for dessert.

On entering, the Moorman saluted his sister-in-law with a low bow. Then he began to shed tears and to question her.

"Where is the place where my brother used to sit?"

She showed it to him. At that he went up to it and began to pray. And he kissed the floor, crying, "O my brother! O vein of my eye!"

4

After such fashion he went on weeping and wailing till he swooned away. Aladdin's mother ran to him and raised him up from the floor. "What gain," she said, "is there in slaying yourself?"

"O wife of my brother," he answered, "it must be a wonder to you how in all your days you never saw me. Now the reason is that forty years ago I left this town and wandered forth over all the lands of Al-Hind and Al-Sind till at last I went to the regions of the Setting Sun. For a space of thirty years I lived in the Moroccan interior. Now one day, O wife of my brother, as I was sitting at home, I fell to thinking of my birthplace and of my brother. 'O man,' I said to myself, 'how long will you wander like a wild Arab far from the place of your birth? Moreover, you have one brother and no more. So up with you and travel and look upon him ere you die.' So I arose. And the day before yesterday I beheld my brother's son Aladdin playing with the boys. And by God the Great, O wife of my brother, the moment I saw him, this heart of mine went forth to him. And my soul told me that he was my own nephew. So I was like to fly for joy. But when he told me of the dear one's departure, I fainted for disappointment. But O my son Aladdin," he continued, "what have you learned in the way of work? Tell me, have you mastered any craft so you can earn a living for yourself and for your mother?"

The lad hung his head.

"By Allah," his mother spoke out, "he knows nothing at all. A child so ungracious as this I never yet saw. No, never! All the day long he idles away his time with scamps like himself. And his father died for grief over him."

The Moorman turned to Aladdin. "Why is this, O son of my brother?" he asked. "You are a youth of sense. 'Tis a shame that your mother should work hard to support you. Look around you and choose some calling. If you dislike a craft, I will open a merchant's store for you. It shall be furnished with costliest stuffs. And you shall take and give and buy and sell and be well known in the city."

Now when Aladdin heard this, he was happy. And the Moorman, seeing him smiling, understood that the lad wanted to become a merchant. So he said to him: "O son of my brother, prove yourself a man and—God willing—tomorrow I will take you to the Bazaar. I will have a fine suit of clothes cut out for you, such as merchants wear. And then I will look after a store for you."

Now Aladdin's mother had doubted that the Moroccan was her brother-in-law. But as soon as she heard him promise to open a merchant's store for her son, she decided that this Moor was in very truth her husband's brother. So she bade Aladdin obey his good uncle as though he were his son.

After this they all sat down and fell to eating and drinking. And when the Moorman saw that the dark hours were passing by, he arose and sped to his own place.

The Enchanted Treasury

Now as soon as it was dawn, behold! the Magician returned. He took the lad to the Bazaar. There he entered a shop and bought for Aladdin a suit of the finest clothes, ready sewn. Presently he led the boy to the Baths, where they bathed. When they came out, they drank sherbets. Then the Magician took Aladdin to the Merchants' Bazaar and showed him its sellings and buyings.

"O my son," he said, "it befits you to know the merchants. For you must learn their craft, seeing that it is now your calling."

Then he led Aladdin forth and showed him the city and its mosques, and all the pleasant sights. And lastly they entered a cook's shop. Here they dined well. After that they went their ways to the Sultan's Palace. And finally they came to the inn of the stranger merchants where the Magician himself was staying. There they sat down to supper. And when night had fallen, the Magician rose up and led the lad back to his mother.

She no sooner saw her boy dressed as a merchant than she grew sad for very gladness.

"O wife of my brother," the Moorman said to her, "Aladdin is now a man of sense. And I hope to Allah that he will follow in the footsteps of his sire and cool your eyes. I regret that tomorrow, being Friday, I shall not be able to open his shop. But I will come and take Aladdin for a pleasant stroll to the gardens of the city which he may not have seen."

Early next morning the Magician rapped at the door. He took Aladdin's hand, and they went forth together to the gardens beyond the city gate. Aladdin was mad with delight at seeing sights he had never seen in all his born days. And the Moroccan, telling him many a tale, both true and false, drew the lad from garden to garden till at last they left all behind them. And they reached the base of a high and naked hill.

Then Aladdin said, "O uncle mine, whither are we going? I am ready to fall with weariness. There are no gardens before us. So let us hark back and return to town."

"No, O my son," said the Magician. "This is the right road. Rest now. And when you are rested, arise and seek some wood chips and dry fuel sticks with which we may kindle a fire. And I will show you marvelous matters whose like no one in the world ever saw."

Now when the lad heard these words, he forgot he was tired. He fell to gathering sticks till the Moorman cried to him, "Enough, O son of my brother."

Presently the Magician took incense and burned it. And he conjured, murmuring words none might understand. And the ground at once split apart, and there was thick gloom and earthquake and thunder. Aladdin was so frightened that he tried to fly. But the African Magician gave him such a blow that his back teeth were nearly knocked out, and he fell swooning to the ground.

After a time he came to. "O my uncle," he cried, weeping, "what have I done to deserve such a blow as this?"

Then the Moor fell to soothing him. "O my son," he said, "if you do all I shall bid you, you shall become wealthier than any of the kings."

With that he pointed to a marble slab in which was fixed a copper ring. "Under yon stone lie riches of immense value," he said. "They are stored in your name. So set your hand upon the ring and raise the slab. For only you have the power to open it. Nor may any mortal save yourself set foot within this Enchanted Treasury."

At this poor Aladdin forgot his weariness and the blow and his tears. He pulled up the slab. And as soon as the stone was raised, he threw it aside. And there appeared before him a staircase of some twelve stairs.

Then the Magician said: "Go down with all care into that underground until you reach the bottom. There you will find four halls. In each of these you shall see four golden jars, but beware lest you touch them. Do not even allow your gown to brush the jars or the walls. Leave them and go on until you reach the fourth hall. There you will find a door. Open it and pass through into a garden adorned everywhere with fruit-bearing trees. Beyond it you will come upon an open chamber. Therein you will see a ladder of some thirty rungs. And you shall find there a Lamp hanging from the ceiling. Mount the ladder and take the Lamp and place it in your breast pocket after pouring out its contents. And on the way back you are allowed to pluck from the trees what you please. For all is yours so long as the Lamp is in your hand."

With that the Moorman drew off a seal ring and put it on the lad's forefinger. "O my son," he said, "verily this signet shall free you from all hurt and fear which may threaten you."

So Aladdin arose and went down into the underground, where he found the four halls, each with four jars of gold. These he passed by as the Moroccan had bidden him. Then he went into the garden and walked along its length. And he mounted the ladder and took the Lamp and placed it in his breast pocket. Presently he returned to the garden.

Now he had not noticed as he went in, but all these trees bore costly gems for fruit. They were of every color. And the sparkle of the gems paled the rays of the morning sun. But as the lad had never seen things like these, he fancied that all these jewels were of glass or crystal. And he said, "I will collect some of these glass fruits for playthings at home."

So he crammed his pockets full and placed other fruits in his waist-shawl. Then he hurried his pace for fear of his uncle. And he came to the stairs and climbed up till only the last step remained. But this step he found higher than all the others. And he was unable to mount it. So he said to the Moorman, "O my uncle, lend me your hand and help me to climb."

But the Moorman answered, "O my son, give me the Lamp and lighten your load."

"O my uncle," the lad answered, "lend me a hand. And as soon as I reach ground, I will give it to you."

Now the Magician, who wanted the Lamp and nothing but the Lamp, began to insist upon Aladdin giving it to him at once. But the lad could not reach the Lamp on account of the gems which were on top of it in his pocket. Again and again the Wizard demanded what the lad was unable to give. And at last, when the Moorman saw that Aladdin would not hand the Lamp over, he grew terribly angry. He conjured and cast incense in the midst of the fire. And by the might of his magic he caused the lid to replace itself and the earth to close over Aladdin's head. And he left the lad to die of hunger and went his ways and returned to his own land, Africa.

Mystery of the Ring
and the Lamp

Now when the earth was heaped over him, Aladdin began shouting to the Moorman to let him out. But he cried in vain. There was none to answer. And at that moment he understood that the man was no uncle but a liar and a Wizard. Then the unhappy lad despaired of life and fell to weeping. After a while he went down the stairs to see if Allah had left any door open for him. But they were all shut fast, even the door into the garden. So at last, weeping like one who has lost his every hope, he came back to sit upon the stairs.

Now while he sat wailing and weeping, he wrung his hands, praying to Allah. And while he thus implored the Lord, he chanced to rub the Ring which the Magician had placed upon his finger. And behold! a Jinni rose upright before him and cried: "Here am I. Your slave between your hands has come! Ask whatso you want, for I am the slave

13

of him on whose hand is the Ring, the Signet of my lord and master."

The lad looked at him and trembled at the terrible sight. But then he remembered the Moorman's words when giving him the Ring. And he grew brave.

"Ho, you, Slave of the Lord of the Ring," he cried, "I desire you to set me upon the face of the earth!"

Hardly had he spoken when the ground ripped apart, and he found himself in full view of the world. He looked to the right and to the left and recognized the road by which he had come. So he gave thanks to Allah Almighty who had freed him from death. And presently he arose and walked along the way to town and passed on to his own home. Then he went in to his mother and, on seeing her, fell to the ground in a fainting fit. So overcome was he by joy and the memory of past fear.

The widow, who had been moaning and crying for her son three days, hastened to sprinkle water upon his face. And when he came round a little, he prayed her to bring him food.

"O my mother," he said when he had eaten, "learn that this fellow who said he was my uncle is a sorcerer, a liar, a traitor. I think the devils under the earth are not as bad as he. Hear what he did."

Then Aladdin told his mother all that had befallen him. And he drew the Lamp from his breast pocket and showed

14

it to his mother, together with the gems and jewels which he had brought from the garden. But he thought them to be glass or crystal. And then, as he had not slept a wink for three days, he lay down. Nor did he awake till about noon on the second day.

As soon as he shook off sleep, he called for food. But his mother had none to give him. "Wait patiently awhile," she said. "I have spun a trifle of yarn. I will take it to the market street and sell it and buy food for you."

"O my mother," said Aladdin, "keep your yarn. But fetch me the Lamp I brought here that I may go sell it. For it will bring more money than your spinning."

So she fetched it. "But it is very dirty," she said. "After we have polished it, 'twill sell better."

Taking a handful of sand, she began to rub the Lamp. But she had only begun when a Jinni appeared whose face was frightful and whose size was horrible big. And he cried to her: "Say whatso you want of me. Here am I, your Slave and Slave to whoso holds the Lamp. And not I alone, but all the Slaves of the Wonderful Lamp which you hold in hand."

She shook and sank on the ground in a swoon. Now Aladdin was standing afar off. But when he heard the Slave speaking to his mother, he ran and snatched the Lamp from her hand.

"O slave of the Lamp," he cried, "I am hungry and I

"Here am I, your slave."

desire that you fetch me something to eat before I starve."

The Jinni disappeared. But in the twinkling of an eye he returned. In his hands he bore a mighty fine tray of silver. Upon it stood twelve golden platters of meats and dainties, with bread snowier than snow and also two silver cups and two black jugs full of wine. He set all these before Aladdin and vanished from sight.

So they sat down and fell to feeding and tasted for the first time such foods as kings eat. And now his mother would have had him throw away the Lamp. For she said she could never bear a second glance at the Jinni. But Aladdin said it was impossible.

"Its value is priceless," he said. "It befits us, O my mother, to keep this Lamp and take care of it. We must not disclose its mysteries to anyone. And the same is true of the Ring. I will never take it from my finger."

For two full days Aladdin and his mother continued eating of the meats brought them by the Jinni. And when no food was left, Aladdin arose and took one of the platters to the Bazaar. There, seeing a peddler, he offered it to him for sale.

Now the platters were all of the finest gold, but the lad did not know it. So when the peddler gave him a gold piece in exchange, he hastily took it and went his way. And whenever his mother was in need, Aladdin took another platter to the peddler and got a gold piece in exchange.

One day as he went forth to find the peddler, he passed by the shop of an old jeweler, an honest man who feared Allah.

"O my son," the jeweler said to him, "many times I have seen you having dealings with a peddler. Now I fancy you have something for sale. Show it to me and never fear. For I will give you its full price by the truth of Almighty Allah."

So Aladdin brought out the platter. And the goldsmith took and weighed it in his scales. "It is worth seventy gold pieces," he said. "And if you please to take its value, take it."

Aladdin accepted the money. And after this whenever the price of a platter was spent, he would bring another to the honest jeweler.

Badr al-Budur

Now Aladdin and his mother were soon better off. Yet they still lived in their old fashion as middle-class folk. But Aladdin had now thrown off the low habits of his boyhood. He went daily to the market street. There he talked with the merchants and learned all about trade. He likewise went to the Bazaars of the goldsmiths and jewelers. He looked at their precious stones and noted how jewels were sold and bought. Thus he soon became aware that the fruits with which he had filled his pockets in the Enchanted Treasury were neither glass nor crystal but gems rich and rare such as no king possessed. And he found that the biggest stone in the Jewelers' Quarter was not worth his smallest.

Now one day as Aladdin passed along the Bazaar, he heard the crier crying:

"By command of our magnificent master, the King of

19

the Time and the Lord of the Age, let all the folk lock up their shops and stores and go into their houses. For the Lady Badr al-Budur, daughter of the Sultan, desires to visit the Baths. And whoso disobeys the order shall be punished with death. And be his blood upon his own neck!"

When Aladdin heard the crier's words, he longed to look on the King's daughter. And he began to devise a plan. He judged the best thing would be to take his station behind the door of the Baths. So he went at once and hid there.

Now when the Sultan's daughter reached the Baths and was about to enter, she raised her veil and Aladdin saw her face.

"In very truth," he thought, "the Creator has adorned her with beauty and loveliness."

From the moment he saw her, his strength was struck down. The love of the Lady Badr al-Budur got hold of the whole of his heart. And he returned home to his mother as one dazed.

"O my son," his mother said, "what has befallen you? You speak not when I speak to you, you eat not, you sleep not."

And Aladdin said to her, "Let me be!"

However, she would not. "I will send for a doctor," she said.

Thereupon he said: "O my mother, I am well in body. But I have looked upon the Princess Badr al-Budur and

20

The Sultan's daughter raised her veil.

have seen her even as she is. I have resolved to win her, and rest is not possible for me unless I do. Therefore, I intend to ask her to wife from the Sultan her father."

When Aladdin's mother heard this, she cried out that he had lost his senses. "O my son, speak not such speech, lest any overhear you," she said. "Cast away such nonsense! Remember whose son you are, my child, the orphan boy of a tailor, the poorest in the city. How dare you ask to wife the daughter of the Sultan? And who shall undertake a matter like this and make such a request to the King?"

"You shall go to him," Aladdin said.

And she answered him: "How shall I be bold enough to ask for the daughter of the Sultan of China-land? It may be the cause of death for you and me. The King will hold me to be a madwoman. And, suppose I do get speech with the Sultan, what offering can I give him? For whoso goes to the Sultan to ask a favor must take in hand something that suits the royal majesty."

"O my mother," Aladdin replied, "you speak to the point. And it is this that emboldens me to ask the King for his daughter. You say I have no gift which I can give to the Sultan. Yet in very truth I have an offering and a present whose equal, O my mother, none of the kings possesses. No, nor even anything like it. Because verily that which I thought glass or crystal is costliest gems. Compose your mind. We have in our house a bowl of China porcelain.

22

Arise and fetch it, that I may fill it with jewels, which you shall carry as a gift to the King. And if you are not willing to strive for the winning of my wish, know that surely I shall die."

So she brought him the China bowl and set it before her son. And he pulled the stones out of his pockets and laid them in the bowl till he had filled it. And when it was full, she could not fix her eyes firmly on it, but winked and blinked. Such was the dazzle of the stones.

Then Aladdin said: "Now you have seen and have no excuse. So take this bowl and away with it to the palace."

So next day the mother wrapped up the bowl full of jewels in a fine kerchief. And she went forth early that she might reach the audience chamber before it became crowded.

When she passed into the palace, she saw the Wazirs and Lords of the land, Chieftains and Emirs and Grandees, going into the judgment room. After a time the Sultan came and sat on his throne. Then the claimants came before the Sultan. And he judged their cases. And when the audience was ended, the King went to his Harem while the rest went their ways. And Aladdin's mother also returned home.

"O my child, be of good cheer," she said to her son. "Today there were many like myself who could not get a chance to speak to the Sultan. But tomorrow I will speak for your sake."

Next morning she arose and went again with her bowl.

23

But she found the chamber closed. "The King holds a levee only three times a week," they told her. So after this she went whenever she saw the court open. She would go and stand before the King until the audience ended. But she did not have the boldness to come forward and speak even a word. And this was how it was for the whole month.

The Sultan Makes a Promise

The Sultan saw Aladdin's mother at every levee. But she never came forward. Now on the last day of the month, as the King was going to his Harem, he turned to his Grand Wazir and said: "O Wazir, I see a certain old woman at every levee. I also note that she always carries something under her shawl. Do you know what she desires?"

"O my lord the Sultan," said the Wazir, "doubtless she comes here to complain before you against her husband or some of her people."

But this reply did not satisfy the Sultan. And next time when he saw her in the hall, he said to his Grand Wazir: "This is the woman of whom I spoke. Bring her before me at once."

So the Minister obeyed. And Aladdin's mother kissed her finger tips and raised them to her brow. And she kissed the ground before the Sultan.

Thereupon he said: "O woman, for several days I have seen you at the levee without a word said. So tell me if you have any request I may grant."

She kissed the ground a second time. "Yea, verily, O King of the Age," she said, "I have a want. But first of all grant me a promise of safety."

The King gave his word. Then he sent away all those about him save the Grand Wazir. And he said: "Inform me of your suit."

"O our lord the Sultan," she said, "I have a son called Aladdin. And he one day beheld the Lady Badr al-Budur even as she went to the Baths. And since the time he looked upon her, O King of the Age, unto this hour life has not been pleasant to him. And he has required of me that I ask her to wife from your Highness. Nor could I drive this fancy from his mind. So I hope that your Highness will be merciful. Pardon this boldness on the part of me and pardon my child. Do not punish us."

The Sultan looked at her kindly. Then he laughed aloud. And at last he said, "And what may be that which you carry in yonder kerchief?"

She opened the wrapper. And the audience-hall was lighted up by the jewels. And the King was dazed and amazed at the sparkle of the rare gems.

"Never at all until this day," he said, "did I see anything like these jewels for size and beauty. I think there is not

26

"Go tell your son I have given my word."

in my treasury a single one like them." And he said, "Now, indeed, whoso has presented to me such jewels deserves to become bridegroom to my daughter, Badr al-Budur."

When the Wazir heard this, he was tongue-tied with grief. For the King had promised to give the Princess in marriage to his son. So after a little while he said: "O King of the Age, you promised your daughter to my son. 'Tis but right to have a delay of three months. During that time my child may obtain and present an offering yet more costly than this."

The King knew that such a thing could not be done. Yet he granted the delay. Then he turned to Aladdin's mother. "Go to your son," he said, "and tell him I have given my word that my daughter shall be his. Only he must be patient for the next three months."

Aladdin's mother went forth in hottest haste and told the whole tale to her son.

"By Allah," he cried when he had heard all, "up to this time I was in the grave. You have drawn me out. I am at this moment certain that no man in the world is happier than I or more fortunate." And he took patience until two months had gone by.

Midnight Adventures

Now one day Aladdin's mother went forth after sundown to the Bazaar to buy oil. And she found the shops shut and the whole city decorated. Also she saw soldiers on guard. So she asked why. And one answered her: "Know you not that this very night the son of the Grand Wazir goes to the Lady Badr al-Budur? The marriage contract has been signed. He is now in the Baths, and the soldiers are on guard to await his coming forth. Then they will bear him in bridal procession to the Sultan's palace where the Princess awaits him."

Aladdin's mother ran home to her son. "Verily," she cried, "the Sultan has broken his promise to you in the matter of the Lady Badr al-Budur." And she told him all.

At first Aladdin was seized with a fever of grief. "It is too late, too late," he told himself. "The marriage contract has been signed. Already the Wazir's son is bridegroom to the

29

Lady Badr al-Budur, and even now the soldiers are bearing him in procession to the palace to pay his first visit to the bride."

Aladdin's soul was filled with jealousy thinking of the Wazir's son and Badr al-Budur alone together in their own quarters at the Sultan's palace. But then he remembered the Lamp. Going to his chamber, he brought it out and rubbed it. And at once the Jinni appeared.

"Ask whatso you want," he cried, "for I am your Slave and Slave to him who holds the Lamp in hand—I and all the Slaves of the Lamp."

"Hear me!" Aladdin answered. "When you shall see the Sultan's daughter and her bridegroom bedded this night, take them up and bring them here. This is what I want of you."

So in the night, behold! the Jinni came. And in his hands he bore the newly wedded couple upon their bridal bed.

Then Aladdin cried to the Slave, "Carry that gallows-bird out and lock him up till morning."

So the Slave took away the trembling bridegroom and locked him in a closet. And Aladdin said to Badr al-Budur, "Princess of fair ones, your father promised you to me. But think not that I brought you here for harm. Rest in peace."

However, the Lady Badr al-Budur passed the worst of all nights, as indeed did the bridegroom too. And in the morning when the Slave appeared, Aladdin said, "Go, carry the bride and bridegroom to their own apartment."

"Think not that I brought you here for harm."

So the Slave bore away the pair and placed them in the palace as they were. And nobody saw the Jinni at his work.

Scarcely had he done this when the Sultan came to kiss his daughter good-morning and ask her if she was pleased with her bridegroom. But she looked sour. She gave him no answer at all, nor could he get her to say a word. So he sent the Queen to her to see what she could do. And the Queen said, "O my daughter, let me know what the trouble is."

Then the Lady Badr al-Budur told her all. But the Queen said it was her fancy. "Say nothing like that to anyone," she said, "for they will think you are mad." And she ordered the women to dress the Princess for the marriage festivities.

All that day the Lady Badr al-Budur sat in silence while the festivities went on. And when darkness fell, everything happened just as on the night before.

Now in the morning the King came again. And again his daughter only glowered at him. Then the Sultan grew angry. He bared his sword and cried, "Either tell me what happened or this very moment I will take your life!"

At that the Princess told him what had befallen her the past two nights. "If you do not believe me," she ended, "ask my bridegroom."

So the Sultan called for the Grand Wazir. And the Grand Wazir questioned his son. And the end of it was that the marriage was dissolved.

Aladdin Gets His Heart's Desire

Now Aladdin waited patiently until the three months had passed. Then he sent his mother to the Sultan to require him to keep his promise.

When the King saw the old woman standing in the audience chamber, he remembered his promise. And he sent the Wazir to fetch her before him first of all.

"O King of the Age," she said when he asked her what she wanted, "it is time to marry my son Aladdin with your daughter, the Lady al-Budur."

The Sultan looked at her poor clothing, and he was dismayed. "In very truth," he said to the Grand Wazir, "I did give my word. Yet it seems to me they are not persons of high standing. What can I do?"

The Grand Wazir, who was dying of envy, said: "O my lord, 'tis an easy matter to keep off a poor devil such as this. Demand of him forty platters made of pure gold and full

33

of gems—such as the woman brought before. And demand forty slave girls to carry the platters and forty men slaves to escort them."

"By Allah," the King answered, "you have spoken well. For such a thing is not possible, and we shall be freed."

And he made his demand.

Aladdin's mother came home all shaking. "O my son," she said, "did I not tell you that such a matter as the Lady Badr al-Budur is not possible to folk like ourselves?"

"Tell me what happened," he said.

So she told him the King's demand. But Aladdin only laughed. "Compose yourself, O my mother," he said. "I thought he would ask much more. Go out and buy what we need for dinner, and by and by you shall see my reply."

So she went out. Then Aladdin took the Lamp and rubbed it. And when the Jinni appeared, he gave him commands. And presently the Slave returned, bringing the platters and jewels and a whole procession of handmaids and men slaves.

When his mother came home, Aladdin said to her, "This is your time to go before the Sultan."

He arose and opened the house-door. And the handmaids and men slaves went forth in pairs, each girl with a man beside her. And Aladdin's mother went before them. All the folk of the ward stood gazing at the marvelous sight. And the citizens gathered to gaze at the beauty of the girls and the loveliness of their robes, all embroidered with gold.

When they stood before the Sultan, they all saluted him. Then they set the platters of jewels at his feet and rested with arms crossed behind them. The Sultan gazed at the marvel like the dumb. He could not utter a word for wonder.

Then Aladdin's mother came forward. "O my lord," she said, "this is not much to honor the Lady Badr al-Budur, for she deserves these things many times over."

The King turned to the Grand Wazir. "What say you?"

Envy was killing the Wazir. So he made answer thus: " 'Tis not worthy of her. O my liege, all the treasures of the world are not worth a nail-paring of your daughter."

But the Sultan saw that envy was behind the words. So he said, "O woman, go to your son and tell him to come to me at once that I may become acquainted with him. And this night the marriage festivities shall begin."

Aladdin's mother went home with the speed of the storm-winds. And she told him the Sultan's words. "And now, O my son," she said, "the rest is on your shoulders."

Aladdin kissed his mother's hand and thanked her. Then he went into his chamber and took the Lamp and rubbed it, and behold! its Slave appeared and cried, "Here am I. Ask whatsoever you want."

"It is my desire," he said, "that you take me to the Baths. Then fetch me a dress so costly and kingly that no king ever had one like it."

"I hear and I obey," the Jinni replied to him instantly.

So Aladdin was washed and bathed and dressed. And he mounted a stallion whose like was not amongst the Arabian Arabs. Then he sent for his mother and gave her rich garments to wear and twelve slave girls to go with her to the palace. And he rode forth with two dozen Mamelukes on war horses going before and behind. And they scattered gold amongst the crowd.

At the door of the audience chamber, Aladdin got down. Emirs and Nobles led him to the royal throne. The Sultan came down from his seat and embraced and kissed him and seated him beside himself. And Aladdin did and said

all things that were fitting, as though he had been bred in the palaces of the kings. And the Grand Wazir burned with envy until he was like to die.

Now when the marriage contract was written, Aladdin said: "O my lord the King, it is my wish to build for the Lady Badr al-Budur a pavilion befitting her high rank. Nor can I visit her before I do it. But the building shall be finished within the shortest time."

"I think," said the Sultan, "the best ground for you will be yonder broad plain facing my palace."

"And this," answered Aladdin, "is just what I desire, that I may be near your Highness."

37

A Pavilion for Badr al-Budur

So saying, Aladdin took horse and rode home and rubbed the Lamp. And behold! the Slave stood before him.

"Build me," Aladdin said, "a pavilion facing the palace of the Sultan. And make it a marvel in every respect."

"To hear is to obey," the Jinni answered and vanished.

Before dawn he returned to Aladdin and took him to inspect the pavilion. And Aladdin looked and was wonderstruck. For the building was all jasper and alabaster and marble. And all within was a marvel in every respect.

When Aladdin had seen all, he said: "I require one thing more. I want a carpet that shall stretch from here to the Sultan's palace. The Lady Badr al-Budur shall not tread common earth."

The day was brightening now. So the Sultan rose from sleep. As he looked out upon the palace grounds, he fell to

38

A carpet stretched to the palace.

rubbing his eyes. For behold! across from the palace was a pavilion. And a carpet stretched from it to the palace.

The Wazir had come in meantime. "Have you seen now," said the Sultan, "that Aladdin is worthy to be the husband of the Princess my daughter?"

But the Wazir in his envy replied, "O King of the Age, indeed this building may not be save by means of magic."

Aladdin led the Sultan all through the pavilion. The King marveled greatly at all. But especially he was struck by the skylights and latticed windows, for they were made wholly of rubies and other costly gems. Now by chance the Sultan noticed one window which Aladdin had purposely left unfinished. "What is the reason for it?" the Sultan asked his son-in-law.

"O King of the Age," Aladdin answered, "my wedding was so sudden that I failed to find artists to finish this window."

"I have a mind to finish it myself," the Sultan said. So he called in jewelers and goldsmiths and told them to take all the gold and gems they needed from the treasury. So they fell to work and worked months on end. But before they were half done, they had run out of jewels. Then Aladdin caused all their work to be undone and commanded the Slave of the Lamp to finish the window in a single night. And it was done.

The Magician Returns

Such, then, was the high fortune of Aladdin. But to turn now to the Magician, who had left him underground to die.

One day as the Moorman was doing his Black Magic, he learned that Aladdin was not dead. Moreover, he found out that the lad he had left to die had become owner of the Lamp. At that the Magician's wrath knew no bounds. And he said, "I shall destroy him."

At once he set off for China and made for the capital.

Now when the Moorman saw the pavilion of Aladdin, he knew that it was the work of the Lamp. And through his magic arts he learned that the Lamp was in the pavilion and not on Aladdin himself. "Now, indeed, it will be easy," he said, "to take Aladdin's life. And I see my way to getting the Lamp."

So first he went to a coppersmith and bade him make

him some lamps. Then he put the lamps into a basket and began wandering about the highways of the city. "Ho!" he cried. "Who will exchange old lamps for new lamps?"

When folk heard him cry this, they made fun of him. "This man is mad," they said. And a crowd of children followed him, laughing. But he kept on strolling and crying his cry. And when he came to Aladdin's pavilion, he shouted in his loudest voice while the boys screamed at him, "A madman! A madman!"

Aladdin was away from home. And it chanced that the Lady Badr al-Budur was sitting in her apartment with her handmaidens. She heard one crying like a crier and the children bawling at him. Only she did not understand what was going on. So she gave orders to one of her slave girls: "Go and see who is crying and what is his cry."

The girl laughed when she heard the man crying, "Ho! Who will exchange old lamps for new lamps?" And the Princess laughed just as hard when this strange matter was told to her.

Now Aladdin had carelessly left the Lamp without locking it up in his strongbox. And one of the slave girls who had seen it said, "O my lady, I think I noticed in the apartment of my lord Aladdin an old lamp. So let us give it in exchange for a new lamp to this man and see if his cry be truth or a lie."

The Princess agreed, for she knew nothing about the Lamp. So the handmaid brought it, and the Lady Badr al-Budur sent a man down to trade it. Soon he returned with a new lamp. And the Princess fell to laughing at the silly Moorman who had so clearly lost his wits.

But the Magician had at once recognized the Lamp of the Enchanted Treasury. At once he left all the other lamps to the folk in the street. And he ran till he was clear of the city. And when night came, he brought out the Lamp and rubbed it, and the Jinni appeared.

"It is my desire," the Magician commanded, "that you raise up Aladdin's pavilion, with all that are in it, and me too, and set it down in my gardens in my own land, Africa."

Aladdin in Distress

Now it was the custom of the Sultan every morning, when he had shaken off sleep, to open the window and look out toward Aladdin's pavilion. So that day he rose and looked and saw nothing. The site was smooth as a well-trodden road. In vain he rubbed his eyes. Then tears trickled down his cheeks and beard. For he knew not what had become of his daughter. Then he sent for the Grand Wazir and bade him look out.

"O King of the Age," the Wazir cried when he saw the pavilion gone, "long ago I said it was all magical."

"Where is Aladdin?" the Sultan demanded in a mighty rage.

"He has gone à-hunting," the Wazir said.

Then the King ordered his son-in-law to be brought before him, bound and chained. So the army officers went and found him and put chains on him and bound his arms

44

behind his back. And when they arrived with him at the palace, the Sultan commanded the Sworder to cut off Aladdin's head. But Aladdin was so beloved by the soldiers and the people that they would not let him be harmed. The people swarmed up the walls, intending to tear them down. So the Sultan bade the Sworder stay his hand from Aladdin. And he pardoned his son-in-law.

All this time Aladdin did not know what the matter was nor what had caused the Sultan's anger. But finding himself free, he went in to the King as he sat on his throne. And he said, "O my lord, let me know how I have sinned against you."

"O traitor!" cried the King. Then turning to the Wazir, he said, "Take him and make him look out at the window and let him tell us where his pavilion is."

Aladdin looked and saw the place level as a well-trodden road. Nor was there the faintest trace of a building. He was amazed and did not know what had happened.

"What have you seen?" the King demanded. "Where is your pavilion and where is my daughter, the core of my heart, my only child and I have no other?"

"O King of the Age," Aladdin said, "I know naught of what has happened."

"Understand O Aladdin," the King said, "that I have pardoned you only that you should go and look into this affair. Never show yourself in my presence unless my daughter is with you. And if you do not bring her, I will cut off your head."

"To hear is to obey," Aladdin said. "But let me have forty days. If I have not found the Princess in that time, do with me whatso you wish."

"Verily," the Sultan said, "I have granted your request— a delay of forty days. But do not think you can fly from my hand. For I would bring you back even if you were above the clouds."

"O my lord the Sultan," Aladdin replied, "if I fail to bring her within forty days, I will present myself for my head to be struck off."

Aladdin's Revenge

So saying he went away and wandered two days about the city as one who has lost his wits. And on the third day he left the city to stray about the open and waste lands outside the walls. He had not a notion as to where he should go. Walking by the river, he gave way to despair. He thought to cast himself into the water. Then he clasped his hands in his grief, and lo! he rubbed the Ring. At once its Slave appeared.

"Here am I," the Jinni cried. "Your slave between your hands has come. Ask of me whatsoever you want."

Aladdin's heart swelled with joy when he saw the Jinni. "O Slave," he cried, "I desire that you bring before me my pavilion and my wife and all therein."

"O my lord," the Slave replied, "you demand of me that which I cannot perform. This matter depends on the Slave of the Lamp. I dare not even attempt it."

47

"Then," said Aladdin, "at least take me up and set me down beside my pavilion in whatsoever land it may be."

Thereat the Jinni lifted him high in the air. And in the space of an eye-glance he set him down beside his pavilion in Africa, upon a spot facing his wife's apartment.

It was nightfall. So, being worn out, Aladdin lay down under a tree close by the building. He slept hard till morning. Then he washed himself and sat down under the windows of the Princess' bower.

Now it happened that the favorite slave girl of the Lady Badr al-Budur looked out of the window in the morning. And she saw her master sitting below.

"O my lady! O my lady!" she cried. "Here is my lord Aladdin seated at the foot of the wall!"

The Princess ran to the window and looked. And her heart leaped within her. She saluted Aladdin and he saluted her. And both were like to fly for joy. And she cried out, "Up and come in to me by the private entrance, for He is not here." And she gave orders to the slave girl, who went down and opened for him. Then Aladdin passed through and was met by his wife.

Now when they had embraced and exchanged kisses with all delight until they wept for joy, Aladdin said: "It is my desire to ask you a question. I had in my apartment an old copper lamp. What became of it?"

Then the Lady Badr al-Budur told him all that had passed

The Jinni lifted Aladdin high in the air.

and also that the Magician came once every day to visit her. "He would woo me to his love," she said. "He would have me forget you and take him for a husband instead. But he never sees anything of me save weeping and wailing. Nor has he heard from me one sugar-sweet word."

"Tell me," Aladdin said, "where has he placed the Lamp?"

"He bears it about his body always," the Princess replied.

Then Aladdin rejoiced. "I will devise a plan to slay him," he said.

With that he went out of the pavilion and changed garments with a poor man and went into a shop and bought a powerful poison. After that he returned to his wife and said: "Hear me! I desire that you dress yourself in your best and cast off all show of care. Also when the Magician visits you, receive him with a 'Welcome and fair welcome.' Meet him with smiling face and invite him to come and sup with you. Moreover, let him believe that you have forgotten me and also your father, and that you have learned to love him with a great love. Then ask him to drink to you in red wine. And when you have given him two or three cups full and have made him grow careless, then drop these drops into his cup and fill it up with wine."

So she adorned herself. And when the Moorman came that night, she met him with welcome and a laughing face. And they ate and drank together. And at the end, when

the wine had mastered his brains and he all but swooned
with love for her, she offered him a cup of wine in which
she had mixed the poison. He suspected nothing. At one
draught he drank off the wine. And immediately he rolled
upon his back like one dead.

Then the Princess sent for her husband. And Aladdin
bade them leave him alone with the Moorman. First he
took the Lamp out of the Magician's bosom. Then he
unsheathed his sword and slew the villain.

And They Lived Happily Ever After

Presently Aladdin rubbed the Lamp and the Slave appeared.

"I desire of you," Aladdin said, "that you take up my pavilion and carry it to the land of China and set it down facing the palace of the Sultan."

Now the Sultan had done nothing but weep for his daughter, his only child. And morning after morning as he shook off sleep, he would hasten to the window and look to where Aladdin's pavilion had stood. On that day he arose and looked out when, lo and behold! he saw the pavilion before him. So he called for his horse and mounted it and made for the place.

And when Aladdin saw his father-in-law coming, he went down and met him half way. Then he led him into the apartment of his daughter.

The King folded Badr al-Budur in his arms and shed

tears of joy. Whereupon she told him all that had befallen her and showed him the body of the Magician. And the King caused it to be burned and its ashes to be scattered in the air.

Next he took to embracing Aladdin and kissing him. "Pardon me, O my son," he said, "for that I was about to destroy you. It was because I had lost my daughter, my only one, who is dearer to me than my very kingdom."

Then the Sultan bade the city to be decorated. A high feast was held. And for full thirty days there were rejoicings in honor of the homecoming of the Lady Badr al-Budur and her husband Aladdin.

So Aladdin lived with his wife in all pleasure and joy. And after a while, when the Sultan died, his son-in-law was seated on the throne. He commanded and dealt justice to all. So the folk loved him. And he lived out his life in comfort and happiness.

Legacy Books